TRUST

BEING THERE FOR EACH OTHER

PRIYA GOPAL

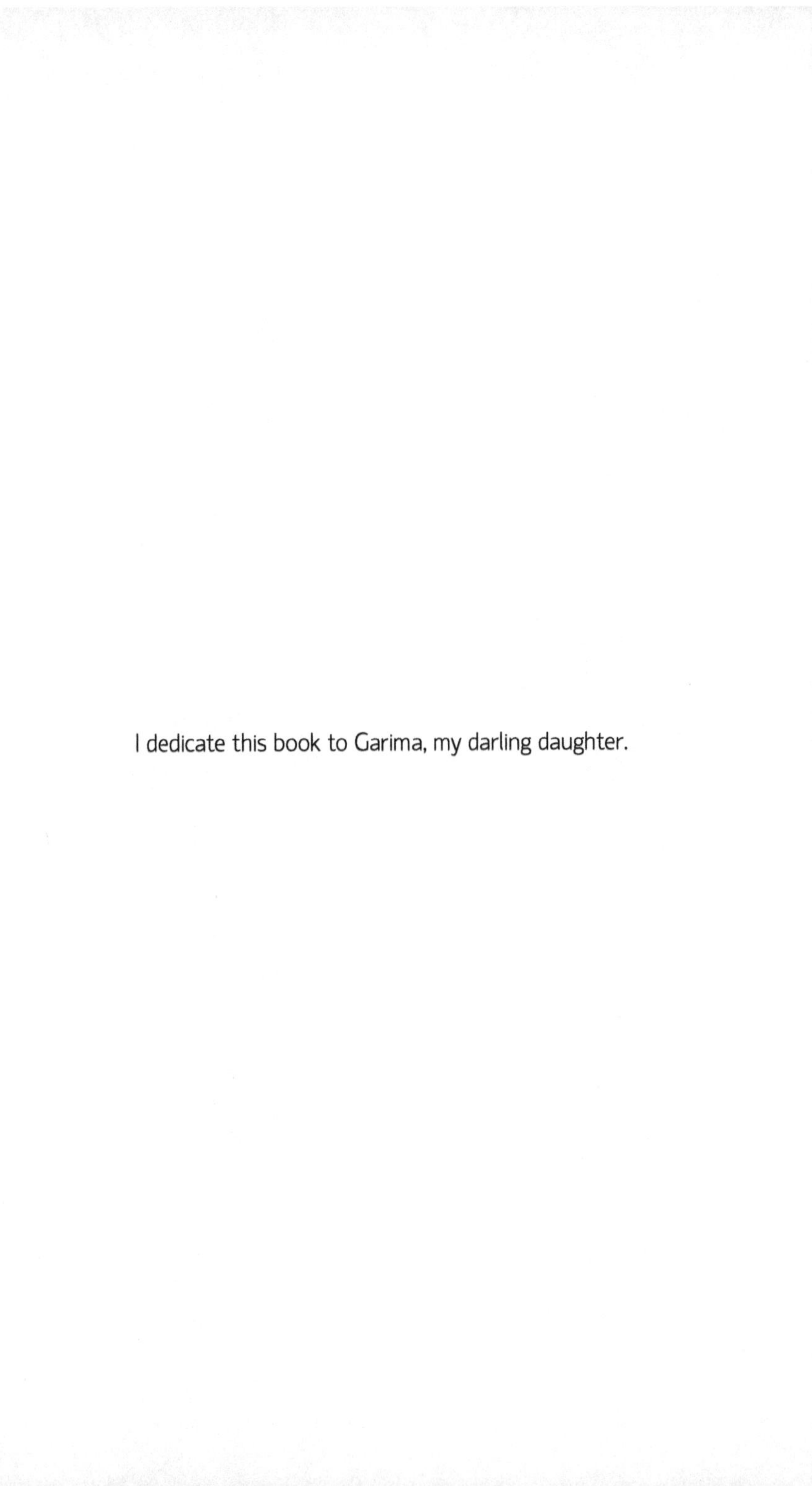

I dedicate this book to Garima, my darling daughter.

Contents

Foreword

This book has got its foundations in the sacred feeling called trust. Lack of family, education, discipline or bad habits doesn't mean the end of the world or Depression. Just the three feelings- trust, respect and care can do magic. This book is on a positive note.

Preface

Unlike many of my earlier works, this book has got a single story divided into three parts. Each part is a literary medicine for people who complain of bad-luck, no money, lack of education or no parents to support them.

The basic characters are:

Rishabh- The spoilt rich brat. He's a college dropout who had an array of bad habits. He was aimless.

Latika- Rishabh's father's late bodyguard's daughter who is one year younger to him and is a successful lawyer.

John Madison- Latika's american husband who is a perfect match for her.

Avantika- Initially a CA intern, who moves from being a girlfriend to a caring wife to Rishabh.

This book is my second one in the paperback version, the first one being 'Horror Stories vol 4'. I've written fourteen ebooks: 'Smiles of the concrete city part 1, 2, 3, 4 and 5', 'Guys we love you', 'All for you dad', 'The smart divorcee', 'Teenage: the wonder years', 'Genius minds', 'Thrillers at their best vol 1, 2 and 3' and 'Horror stories vol 1, 2 and 3'. Other than this I've also written four serial stories: 'Vinod and Mrinalini', 'Vishal and Yogita', 'Vivek and Mohini' which explored the depths of marital love in today's world and 'Kriti and Shruti' based on teenage life of two sisters and their preparations for a strong and independent adult life.

Acknowledgements

I thank my husband for putting up with my erratic work schedules. I thank my daughter Garima for being my honest critic and my father for supporting me in every way possible.

PART 1

Chapter 1

"Latika, I trust only you. I've seen you grow up. You are like my child only. I'm having just one regret while now when I'm dying. All my friends' kids are doing well, but my son... my son is the only one... the only one who is spoilt to death. Gambling, prostitutes, drugs, alcohol, cigarettes every bad habit in the world he is having. He is not taking any responsibility. He is immature and heading towards doom. I can't do the property, bank-balance and company in his name. Money and power will spoil him further. Even though he is one year older to you, you are in a thousand ways better than him, so what if you are born from another mother's womb ? So I have spoken to advocate Ramnath Oberoi and given the 'power of attorney' in your name. After my death, don't call up my ex-wife, she's... she's HIV +tive now. She informed this to me four years ago. She got this from the man she left me for. Its God's way of punishing her for ruining... ruining my and her own son Rishabh's life. Please... please take care of my son" explained an emotional Mr Giridhar Batra. "I'll take care of your son. I will take good care of him. I promise... I promise. You don't take tension uncle. Tension will ruin your health even more." A good soul, Latika gave him the assurance he needed. He smiled and became still. The monitor started showing a horizontal line continuously without stopping. The doctor who stood next to her, took charge. He frantically checked a few details and confirmed that the patient was no more.

Rishabh was ofcourse a thoroughly spoilt brat with all the vices in the world, but he respected Latika. She was his father's trusted bodyguard Mahadeo Sawant's daughter. She was one of the top lawyers in Mumbai. The cremations took place with Latika and her mother standing next to Rishabh. All through the final rites, Latika didn't allow him to touch even a single bottle. After all the cremation procedures were totally over, Rishabh was shifted to her house with four-bedrooms in a posh tower. She called up her american husband John Madison and explained everything in a very detailed manner. On her advice, he resigned from his plush job over there and came to Mumbai. He took over as the CEO and MD of Mr Giridhar Batra's company. Rishabh didn't feel bad at all, since now he thought he'd get more time for his vices and no one was going to nag him.

There were five members in Latika's house now. Latika, her husband, her mother Janki, Rishabh and servant and cook Rajesh. Latika kept Rishabh under observation. This is because she didn't want him to go back to his initial vices. She took whatever his father told her very seriously. All the members of the house were instructed in advance that if possible they should try to inculcate healthy habits in Rishabh and that the owner of the house ie Latika doesn't want him to basically, go back to his initial vices.

The family always had breakfast together. And John made it a point to see TV with Rishabh daily before going to bed. For Rishabh, who had a very concerned father, but never the warmth and discipline of a home with family, this came as a breath of fresh air. A week passed, Latika liked the smiling face of Rishabh now.

While having breakfast, Rishabh asked Latika "I love the way Rajesh cooks food. All the past week he prepared simple Indian food which were mouthwatering. So, Latika I want to learn cooking from him. I want to become expert in all the indian delicacies. I want to make the perfect paratha, butter-chicken, payasam... mmm... all of these. I'm telling seriously that I want to learn cooking". Latika smiled and said "Okay, he'll teach you. Expertise, that's really good". So from the right next day, Rajesh began his cooking classes with student Rishabh. Rishabh initially noted down the cooking notes in his late dad's laptop and began practically learning as well.

During dinner, John asked Rishabh whether he'd like to see Bruce Lee's film 'Enter the dragon' with him. Rishabh said "Okay" to it. For the next one week, both the men saw movies after dinner and enjoyed thoroughly.

Then during breakfast one day, Rishabh asked Latika "Latika, I feel I feel from my heart that I should join Karate classes. I've already spoken to John, I also saw the banner 'Enter China Kung Fu classes' in sector 16. Should I join it ?" Latika smiled and again said "yes".

The cooking classes and Kung Fu classes began. Latika was happy since now, Rishabh was doing something that was healthy.

Five years passed. With a healthy and loving lifestyle, Rishabh got his black belt in Kung Fu and also cooked all the north Indian, south Indian, Mughlai and Maharashtrian dishes very well. He had the same expertise as Rajesh now. Latika and John didn't put undue pressure on Rishabh and never insulted, compared or belittled him.

Once, Latika and John celebrated their wedding anniversary, just the two of them, in a candle-light dinner in a posh restaurant. When they were returning home in his car, which he was himself driving, John said "Why don't we arrange a dhaba for Rishabh ? His birthday is next month, and I strongly feel he should be doing that. Last week he prepared alu-ke-parathe and I cannot forget the taste. I'm very sure he'll do a great job at it." John advised his wife. On his birthday it was the gift the couple gave him. He was only too overwhelmed. So the dhaba began with just Rishabh and three servants. The main cook was Rishabh himself. It was just next to the busy railway station. It was named 'Rishabh's dhaba'.

Chapter 2

Right from the third month itself the dhaba, started its success spree. Rishabh put his heart and soul in it. Three more months passed and like always, when they were having breakfast together, Rishabh shared with Latika and John the happy news that the Dhaba was doing good business. Latika got emotional. But she didn't show before the others. When she went out of the house with John for their respective work-places, in the parking lot, she hugged her husband and cried. "Finally, my efforts paid off. Rishabh's father may have been happy today, if he was alive. He may be looking from heaven and smiling. Its such a good news" said an overjoyed Latika to him. John too smiled and comforted her.

The next day, on a table in his dhaba, Rishabh was busy searching for a particular Mexican dish. As he scrolled down the laptop screen, someone tapped his shoulder from behind. He turned back. To his amazement, he saw Nisha. She was his classmate from school. Although they never spoke to each other then, but now was a pleasant surprise.

"You recognise me ? I was in school with you." She was a nice girl. Both of them had lunch together that day. While having lunch, he spoke "Its my own Dhaba now. After getting expertise in cooking, this was the next step. God bless Latika and John. They have been my nice pillars of support". "I've done my BAMS. I'm an Ayurvedic Doctor. My clinic is just round the corner" shared Dr Nisha Sabarwal. "Are you married ?" asked Rishabh the next question. Nisha had moist eyes, she answered "I... I'm not married. I'm a divorcee. My husband and in-laws plotted to eliminate me for my expensive jewellery. I had a jewellery box full of gold, diamond and ruby jewellery. Four months after marriage, my sister-in-law happened to see it. The next moment itself, my sister-in-law, mother-in-law, father-in-law and... and even my husband asked for it turn-by-turn. I flatly refused. Then there was even a police case. The police themselves came to the hospital where I was admitted. They told me that my in-laws and my husband tried to poison me for that. The police-woman Nandita Yeole helped me immensely at that time. After getting discharged from hospital where I was for full one week, divorce was the only way out. My parents were supportive. But... but I loved my husband very much. So it was very painful for me. I shifted to a rented apartment, just four months ago. I've a dog Mandy for support." "Any plans to marry again ? Look what if God sends another man for you ?" asked he. Wiping a tear, Nisha answered "The divorce left a bitter taste in my mouth. I don't plan to marry again. I had given my everything, entire love of my heart to my ex-husband. But this is what he's done. I'll never marry again". The tasty potato bhajiya did the trick and cheered up Nisha, she asked him "Are you married ?". He answered with a confident smile "It's a long story. Latika and her husband

John are my family now. She is the firm rock in my life. About marriage... about marriage I haven't given a thought". She smiled.

Both became good friends. Both had lunch together daily.

Chapter 3

"There is a girl over there, sahib. She's crying continuously. I asked her what she wanted, but she didn't say anything. I asked her to sit on the open table in the corner" said a concerned Satish, the servant of the Dhaba. Rishabh immediately went to meet the lady. He asked her "What happened ? Why are you crying ?" The lady answered "My name is Avantika. Its raining very heavily since early morning, because of which the trains have stopped working. How will I go home ?" "See you can stay in my house. Its just round the corner. But first you stop crying" Rishabh gave an option. She stared back angrily at him. "Its my birthday. My friends and family have already arrived at my house for the cake cutting function. But... but how will I join them ? So, I'm crying" Rishabh suggested and coaxed her to blow the candles at his Dhaba itself. The cake was brought from the nearby cake shop. The cake cutting also was done over there. She was happy. Just then, her mobile rang. It was her boss. He conveyed to her over the phone that all the employees of his CA firm could spend the night in the office premises itself. There were arrangements made over there to help the employees like her who stayed faraway. She happily went back. Rishabh was also relieved. But she remembered him and his great gesture. After that day, she and her group of friends frequented the Dhaba. Two months later, she surprised Rishabh by ordering a cake and celebrating his birthday too, right on the Dhaba with her group of friends in full attendance. That day after the party was over, Rishabh sensed something in his heart. He wanted her to turn back once as she walked away and she did turn back, smiled at him and he just jumped with joy. She saw it and walked away. The next day she during lunch in the Dhaba, in front of Nisha expressed to him that she too loved him. She moved her hand towards him. He took it on his hand and kissed the back of her palm and accepted her love with a smile.

The first person to know about this was Latika and John on the breakfast table the next day. Latika asked Rishabh to find out more about the girl. She on her way back from the court that evening went to the nearby temple and prayed to God that the girl should be a good soul who will keep him happy and healthy in the right way. Latika came back home and gave the prasad to all the members of the house. She was concerned about Rishabh.

The next morning, Rishabh like usually, on the breakfast table told them that the girl was doing articleship in a nearby CA firm. She planned to become a CA for which she was working very hard.

Three years passed.

Chapter 4

The friendship between Rishabh and Dr Nisha continued and fluttering of hearts of Rishabh and Avantika also continued.

Then it so happened that for two consecutive days Dr Nisha didn't come to the Dhaba. She was not picking up her mobile also and the clinic was also closed. So to find out what the matter was, Rishabh and Avantika went personally to her house. She opened the door, they came in. But her face was covered with a cloth. She told them that she was suffering from Monkey pox. So she won't be venturing out.

She refused to take help from them. But Rishabh was adamant. He and Avantika shifted to Dr Nisha's house temporarily. Both of them cooked food and also cleaned the house. Till Nisha became hale and hearty again, they continued to help her in every way.

Chapter 5

Latika, John, Avantika, Rishabh, Dr Nisha and Mandy went to Mahabaleshwar for an outing. Latika was suddenly lost for five hours. The others were just searching for her. Then the hotel male staff Devdhar brought an unconscious Latika in his arms to the hotel entrance. Dr Nisha was called. She suggested weakness and prescribed medications and rest for her. Latika-John returned back to Mumbai in their car. John assured Rishabh and Dr Nisha that he'll take full care of her. After three days the others returned back.

Chapter 6

Latika's blood test reported a date rape drug mixed in orange-juice. But who has done it, was the question. It was a police case now. Latika had mid night snacks habit. In the middle of the night, she went out of her room and asked the hotel waiter what they had in food. So the waiter delivered her orange-juice. He asked her to go to the ground floor hotel. Couldn't do room service since all waiters are fast asleep. She went and decided in her mind to share the drink with john half-half. There was an argument with the waiter- he wanted her to drink it over there itself. But she was adamant. She herself brought the big glass full of orange juice to their room. She tried to wake up John but he was fast asleep. So she also dozed off without drinking the juice. First thing in the morning, she was fed-up and so she herself drank the entire juice. Then with the group she went to the restaurant below. She went to the restaurant toilet. But then she didn't remember anything. She directly remembered waking up in the backseat of the car which John was driving. The group especially John was shocked with the blood test report. Police complaint was filed, that waiter was found guilty and he was sent to jail.

Chapter 7

Avantika's dad rejected Rishabh to be his son-in-law since even though his hotel business was good, he was only SSC pass, whereas his daughter was a CA. All pleadings with her father fell into deaf ears.

John's younger sister Lisa came to India for a week long vacation. She was openly reprimanded by John for being a workaholic, although everybody laughed in the end. She was a software engineer working in a top company in the US.

One day at eleven at night, when she was busy working on the laptop, Rishabh made coffee for her and himself and even made some hot kanda bhajiya for her. Driven mad by the aroma, Lisa was impressed. Rishabh struck a conversation with her "My girlfriend's father and elder brother both are engineers. But I'm tenth standard/grade pass. Her father has rejected me very badly. But I have an idea. I'll learn software engineering and become proficient in it and then that old man cannot say no to me." "I understand. But it is not so easy to learn software engineering. It is a full four years course. How can you gain expertise in it just like that ? That's not possible" explained Lisa. "But there are men like Steve Jobs, Bill Gates who are college dropouts like me, but they are still experts and successful in such a difficult and technical subject like computers and mobiles. The problem is not money. Money I have. Look Lisa, I have confidence I'll learn it. You just begin my classes. I'll not let you down I promise" he argued. Lisa just smiled. After four days, Lisa returned back to the US. Two weeks later, there was a parcel in Rishabh's name which he himself received since he was at home. He opened the cover. It was a book titled 'software development from a scratch.' The subtitle ran 'a simple handbook for beginners'. On the back cover of the book a CD with a glittering cover was also attached. Rishabh read the author's name was Lisa Madison. He understood and smiled. It was a self-published book. He thanked God and immediately took out the CD and put it in his laptop. Every day after work for two hours, he went through the book and the CD. For the next eight months this continued. For the next four months he designed various kinds of software for varied types of jobs. He created fourteen softwares, clarifying his doubts with video calls to Lisa herself. He was again confident. And with a smile went on his knees and proposed to Avantika with a diamond ring. She said 'yes'.

Latika and John met Avantika. They loved her and on Latika's advice the couple eloped & got married.

Her brother was fuming with rage. But two weeks after the wedding when they came back, with tears in her eyes, she cajoled her father and brother that he was the one for her. She could never even dream of marrying anybody else. She also asked her brother and father to open their emails and check. Rishabh had sent all twelve softwares which he himself had prepared. After full four days, both father and son, along with Avantika's mom came with a box full of angeer barfi to meet and greet Latika and John. Avantika's dad said "We accept with whole heart our son-in-law Rishabh into the family". He and John hugged.

PART 2

Chapter 1

Avantika was now staying in Latika's house. On the breakfast table, again the discussions began. Latika put forth her opinion "Rishabh, you're a married man now. I want you to buy a new house. Even a small one would do. You should shift over there and live a life of marital bliss with your wife." Rishabh took forward his idea "I'll buy a one BHK in the neighbouring building. I have money. But Latika, I want a take-away facility also at my dhaba. There is huge demand for it. I'm sure it'll be a great success. After I'm successful at that, I spread this take-away system all over Mumbai, Navi Mumbai and Thane district. The target customers are the 9 to 5 office going crowd. I'm sure it'll be a great idea". John said "Okay, even I agree with you. I support it fully." Latika too supported. John gave the money.

Chapter 2

Avantika couldn't understand what was happening. But supported her husband in the end.

Expansion of business brought profits. But sleepless nights too. Rishabh was a total insomniac now. Avantika advised him to not go for sleeping pills, instead he can read books.

His wife also suggested him to read Ravi Arora's books. She also took out a personally autographed copy of his third book from the shelf and showed it to him. So at night when everybody were fast asleep, he started reading the book. It was engrossing. Within two weeks he finished off the book. Then he ordered one more book from online shopping. He was happy that in all there were twenty one books which the author had published. After one year in a dining out together, he told that he was now a self-confessed book lover.

On his wife Avantika's birthday, he gave a surprise to her by inviting Ravi Arora himself to the party. She was pleasantly surprised and overjoyed too. The author was a way too rich man with political connections too. He was also a three times divorcee. He had a weakness for women, which he didn't show before Rishabh. The writer was a man regularly going to prostitutes and led a wine and women kind of a lifestyle.

Chapter 3

He got Avantika's number. He himself called her up for his book-launch function. She without informing him came along with husband Rishabh. After the function was over, both of them returned back home. But the famous author's eyes were cast upon Avantika.

Four months later, she left for office in the morning as usual. But even uptill midnight didn't come back. Rishabh waited and waited. He called her up multiple times. But the phone just rang. She didn't pick it up. He called up all her relatives and friends. But she was not with them. With huge tension mounted on his head, he called up Latika. Latika and John left immediately for Rishabh's house. At morning 7AM sharp Rishabh lodged a complaint with the police.

Two days later, Avantika was found unconscious in a gutter in a faraway place. She was admitted to the hospital. She was in a state of coma. After twenty nine days, she regained her consciousness. Her medical checkup revealed that she was pregnant. On seeing her hale and hearty, he was happy. But was in for a rude shock when he heard the news of her pregnancy. He hugged his wife and he, her and Latika went back to the police station. Avantika with tears in her eyes revealed to the police that she and her husband didn't try for a child at all. That day when she came out of her car in the office parking lot, two men with face covered caught her from behind and the third one made her forcibly snuff a handkerchief. Before she could raise an alarm, she lost her consciousness. Then when she regained her senses, she woke up in the hospital bed with Latika sitting and reading a book calmly beside her. She doesn't remember anything in between. The lie detector test revealed that she was telling the truth. The police were also not able to nab the goons who made her unconscious. Rishabh didn't want her to keep the child. It's either the child or he himself, he made it very clear. Avantika didn't want to go in for an abortion. He pressurised her so much that she started crying. Latika felt bad for Avantika's plight. The later said "Let her give birth to the child. I and John will adopt it". Suddenly Rishabh and his wife turned towards Latika.

Avantika after some months, gave birth to a healthy baby girl. After one month, the baby was legally adopted by Latika and her husband. Latika was so engrossed with baby Sapna that for four full years she took a break from work. Then one year later, Avantika and Rishabh became parents of another baby girl, Amrita.

Chapter 4

At the age of twelve Sapna developed a strange fetish of

cutting out photos of models and actresses. She wanted to learn the art of makeup and repeatedly and continuously watched the videos. A ten thousand rupees worth huge makeup kit along with international brand range of cosmetics were given by John as a birthday gift to her. She was overwhelmed and didn't sleep the entire night because she was busy trying out the twenty seven lipsticks which came along. The next morning, she asked her dad that she wanted to see a fashion show. John also assured her that he'll take her there. Two months later John took her to India's biggest fashion show held in Mumbai itself. The girl was left open-eyed. She clapped her hands with glee and cheered the models as they came on the ramp one after the other. The next morning at breakfast she declared before everyone that she wanted to become a model and this was her career choice. Latika was pleasantly surprised. She said "You can't be a model. There is no guarantee in that line. Don't you read the news that so many models commit suicide because they are not having any money because of lack of work." On the contrary John interrupted saying that "She can become whatever she wants to. I'm there strongly behind her. I'll never allow my girl to fall down." There was a big smile on Sapna's face. By the age of fourteen. She was an expert in makeup and hairstyle. Then she and her father got her portfolio shot and a prestigious modelling agency took on her work. By the age of nineteen she was a top model. Latika was cross. But on her mom's birthday, the dutiful daughter assured her that whenever there will be decline of work for her, she'll leave modelling and resume her studies.

The other little one in the family, Amrita got along like a house on fire with her aunt Lisa Madison's son Mark and firmly decided to be an engineer. She was a confident girl and the apple of her father's eye.

Even though the family had good amount of money, mummy Avantika was very particular about her daughter's academics. She was in fifth grade/standard now. There was a Forbes businessman, who was a former alumni of the same prestigious school, who had promised that every year the top three students in fifth, tenth and twelfth grade will be given scholarships. So the whole attention of Amrita and her mother were fully towards this scholarship. It was hugely prestigious to win that most coveted honour too.

Chapter 5

The day before his birthday, Rishabh came home late. He with a smile said to his wife and daughter that he'll announce the secret venture the next day on his birthday party.

On his birthday party, after cake-cutting he honoured his top three cooks with a gold coin each. The names were selected by customer feedbacks and ratings given by them. Rishabh also announced the non-veg takeaways from then on.

After this birthday celebration, on sundays Amrita started accompanying her dad to his dhaba. She ordered and ate her lunch over there sitting alone on a corner table. It was so good that, she decided to become a cook when she grew up and help her father in handling his food business. As these thoughts crossed her mind, there was a thunder and rain. She thought that in this way, she had God's approval. She smiled and ordered one more samosa.

CHAPTER THREE

PART 3

Chapter 1

Sapna became a successful model and whole world was in awe of her looks. Amrita on the other hand took admission in hotel management degree. After the degree, she started working with her dad. Two months on, she told her dad, he can very much retire and sit at home. Rishabh was impressed the way his daughter handled his food business. Her confidence and a relevant degree and even an 'A grade' in it, floored him. So with a happy feeling, he agreed to sit at home. He explained Avantika about the same. With moist eyes, she directly went to the puja room of their house and thanked God. That saturday, the entire group ie Latika, John, Sapna, Rishabh, Avantika and the apple of her dad's eye- Amrita went to Shirdi. Avantika and Rishabh both closed their eyes and prayed for their daughter's career. After a good darshan they returned back to Mumbai the next day. And from the coming Monday onwards, Rishabh stayed back at home and with full confidence Amrita went to the dhaba.

Now, all forms of food including chaat, momos and chinese food were served over there. It was still basically affordable and good quality food was served there. It catered still basically for the middle class customers. After six months of work, Amrita decided that a first floor and second floor should also be constructed. First floor was supposed to be full AC for the people who believed in splurging their money. It was named 'the maharajas'. On the second floor the marriage hall was planned to be constructed. Work began in full swing. Amrita was excited. The planning was fully implemented. After two years it was inaugurated by her mom Avantika, it started reaping profits. 'Number ghumao, khana pao' was the earlier jingle. Now it was, 'Anniversary ho ya birthday, Maharajas aao har day'. The whole sector was talking about Amrita and her massive feat. She and the maharajas restaurant both became famous. Their restaurant was also covered in one of the episodes of a very promising food channel on television. They also took Amrita's interview. Rishabh was proud of his daughter.

Chapter 2

Then came the massive jolt. At 2 AM at night, the door bell rang. All three of them were fast asleep. But Rishabh got up from bed and opened the door. There were the police outside. They asked for Amrita. Rishabh asked them "She is my daughter. What do you want from her ?". The police man P K Shirke spoke "Five school kids suffered from diarrhea after eating the batata wada in her dhaba. The FIR has been lodged and we have arrest warrant against Amritaji". She was arrested and the entire two storied building was shut by the police. The media covered it. There were tears rolling down Rishabh's eyes as he watched the news in the local channel.

Chapter 3

Later Amrita came out on bail. Latika herself fought her case. Latika first spoke to the fifteen member staff. She told any small information even, should not be hidden or labeled unimportant by the staff, also should be brought to Latika's notice. But nobody came forward. All the five school kids personally testified against Amrita in court. Even the half leftover batata wada piece which was sent to testing in a government laboratory gave its reason stating that the food quality was substandard. So because of eating this, the kids, all five of them had to be admitted to the hospital. The court ordered her to be put in jail and canceled her licences. It was splashed all across the media.

Chapter 4

At six o'clock in the evening Rajiv Mishra, a former employee personally came to Rishabh's posh residence. Rishabh himself opened the door. He told something inside the house. It brought a smile in Amrita's parents' face. They immediately rushed to Latika's house. Even she smiled. The once hopeless case was reopened. The court proceedings began again.

Whatever Rajiv said in the court, everyone listened with rapt attention. There was pin-drop silence. Even the media was there. He testified saying "Amrita and her dad Rishabh are both good people. I've worked with them for six years. What I want you to note is that a certain Mr Shankar Yeole, the man who spoke to me seven months ago, inquired about the dhaba property. He said to me that his boss wanted to buy the two storied property. I directly went inside to Amrita ma'am. She had answered with full confidence that she won't sell the property come what may. And now yesterday morning on local channel, I had seen the same man standing next to Mr Pratap. He was Mr Pratap's man. He was the man who enquired about whether Amrita wanted to sell the big property and that's what I had conveyed to him then and there that ma'am has refused" Latika also added "all five of the kids who testified were studying in the same school, where Dattatray Mhatre was the main trustee. Dattatray Mhatre is the father of Mr Pratap Mhatre who wanted to buy the property. The batata wada were bought as a parcel. Mr Vinayak Kadam who was the servant in Rohit Pundhir's house had eaten up all of the batata wadas himself and replaced it with substandard batata wadas which caused diarrhea to the kids." The police produced Mr Kadam in court and he accepted that he did malpractice and was paid money for doing it by Mr Pratap. The case became crystal clear. Mr Pratap and the other criminals were put behind bars. The media covered the case. And the hotel premises was once again open. The family heaved a sigh of relief.

Chapter 5

As life became normal, there were the new concerns. Latika, John and Sapna went for a holiday in the US. They stayed in Lisa's house over there. After the tense court case a phone call to Avantika from Lisa brought a breath of fresh air. Lisa's son Brady had a bitter break up with his girlfriend and was newly single. So Lisa without wasting any time called up Avantika and asked her daughter Amrita's hand in marriage. The news of Amrita's expertise in handling hotel business and the massive turnover in profits reached America too. Avantika agreed.

Soon in an intimate ceremony in Mumbai, the wedding took place. The groom was a 'firang', which means a foreigner, but he was cute too. He was working in the research and development wing of a top pharmaceutical company over there. Lisa was confident and finally at peace.

Chapter 6

In the wedding Dr Nisha was also invited. She came with her second husband who worked as a manager in a big resort in Kerala where her old group from Mumbai had gone on a vacation. With Rishabh giving her a piece of his mind at the right time, Nisha accepted the manager Shivaprasad's love. After one year Nisha had accepted his marriage proposal and settled down in Kerala. She opened her Ayurvedic clinic over there and was very happy. After the celebrations were over, Latika and John went to see her off at the domestic airport. Just when she was about to go away to board the plane, Nisha whispered in Latika's ears "Just wait for four months. I've something to tell you". Then she went off with a big smile on her face.

Chapter 7

Four months later, Nisha first called up Rishabh and conveyed the good news that her son Mayank had topped the University of Cochin in MS ie master of surgery. Latika finally got a call from Nisha ending all anxiety. Nisha asked Sapna's hand in marriage for her son Dr Mayank Nair. Latika conveyed the real good proposal, to John and Sapna along with the photo of Dr Nair who was no less in good looks, compared to the top model that her daughter was. Sapna liked the photo and after being in a four year long distance relationship with him, finally tied the knot in the same resort where the bridegroom's parents had met for the first time. Nisha felt nostalgic.

"It's just perfect" was the caption given by Dr Nisha, sharing the wedding photos in social media.